THE WILLIAMS FAMILY

presents

In the line of duty

By:K.Moore

Copyright © 2025 by K.Moore

All rights reserved. No part of this book may be used or reproduced in any form whatsoever without written permission except in the case of brief quotations in critical articles or reviews.

This book is a work of fiction. Names, characters, businesses, organizations, places, events and incidents either are the product of the author's imagination or are used fictitiously. Any resemblance to actual persons, living or dead, events, or locales is entirely coincidental.

Printed in the United States of America.

For more information, or to book an event, contact :

relatablefictionwriting@gmail.com

Book design by Nakeia Davis
Cover design by Canva

First Edition: July 2025

Dedication

As an officer of the law it must be in your heart to act in good faith, moral and mental strength to overcome fear, danger, and difficulty.

BOOK TITLE

Prelude

Everyday the officers in this series come across some really crazy stuff. But the difference between them and real life cops is we don't have to put up with Janette. We may know someone like Janette but we call them Karen. The biggest difference between Janette and Karens is Janette will interrogate a person before unleashing her own form of brutality on a suspect.

In this series we'll see how much Janette and her comedic timing will help the guys. Now let's get buckled up for a journey through the daily lives of the officers in Richfield,Tn.

AUTHOR NAME

1

Richfield Seasons Greetings

Dec 13, 2030 Jamal Reynolds was in Richfield to bring Serenity to visit Malcolm. On the way from Antioch Jamal witnessed a car driving erratically across the road. His police skills kicked in and got the vehicle to pull over. When he approached the car there was a woman sitting in the front seat who looked to be intoxicated. Ma'am I'm Officer Reynolds are you ok, Jamal said with concern.
Officer I'm fine I'm just distraught at the thought of the man I love being married to another woman. This is not the way I wanted to spend my birthday, Jamal thought to himself. Ma'am if you're sure you don't need a medic I'll be on my way, Jamal said, turning to walk away. You said you're a cop right , maybe you can help me track someone down that works with the police force. I know a few people on the force in Richfield where I'm headed. Maybe they could help you.

I'm looking for Max Ramirez. He's a cop in Richfield and we belong together, the woman said. Uncomfortable by what he just heard Jamal called Zeek when he got back in the car. **Jamal:** Man I know it's early but can you let Max know some woman is headed to Richfield to find him. **Zeek:** What did she look like? Was she light-skin with short spiky black hair with gothic makeup?**Jamal:** Yeah come to think of it, that's what she looked like. **Zeek:** Dude that's his stalker. That girl has been following him around since we were in the academy. The chief set me, Rashad and Max up on blind dates with some weird chicks. But that one has been trying to ruin Max's life ever since. I'm going to put out a BOLO for her, what did her vehicle look like? **Jamal:** It's a Yellow GMC Acadia and the plate is JLK 1245. I'll be on the lookout while I'm in town.

What are you doing in Tennessee, I thought you'd be in VA with the kids? **Jamal:**Serenity wanted to see Malcolm and have Kapri do her hair. So I'm spending my birthday in Richfield. We'll be heading back on the 24th. **Zeek:** me and the boys will take you out before you head back. Where will you be staying while you are here? **Jamal:** I'll be right across the street with the Stantons so Serenity can get to big brother.

The two men talked for a few more minutes before hanging up. Zeek called the station telling the operator on duty to put out the BOLO for Juanita Lynn Krupa and her vehicle. By morning Zeek was on the phone with Max regarding his situation. The moment Max said "What amI gonna do, man" Cora took the phone and told Zeek she would be handling Juanita personally.

Little did anyone know Juanita had been driving around the city looking for Max's address. By the 24th Jamal spotted her and followed her through the southside where Max lived. When she turned right on Tuscan Row Ct it was then Jamal called Zeek asking for Max's address. **Zeek:** Why do you need his address,man? **Jamal:** I was heading home and saw ole girl watching your house so I followed her. She just turned on Tuscan so I wanted to know if lived over here. **Zeek:** Yeah his house is 2435 Tuscan, watch her I'll send you some backup.

Jamal watched as Juanita parked 3 houses down and walked toward the address Zeek told him. He got out of his truck just as other officers arrived along with Max pulled up. Jamal what are doing at my house shouldn't you be headed home, Max asked confused? Yeah but your stalker has been camped out at Zeek's looking for you so I followed her over here. I think she's gonna hurt your family so we need to get in there quick. In the next second the sound of fighting was coming from the garage.

When Max pressed the remote for the garage the whole neighborhood could see the 5' of fury in Cora raining punches and slaps to Juanita's face and head. It was like watching a mini Janette until Cora took off her flip flops and continued to attack Juanta's face. At one point Cora slapped Juanita with so much force that her head bounced off the rim of the back tire or Cora's car. Once everyone went their separate ways Jamal made his way to Antioch,Va while Max cautiously walked around his home. He never thought his sweet innocent wife would snap like that.

By the next morning Max was not sure who this new version of Cora was . As she walked into the kitchen with the kids in tow she said to him " she got all her gifts handed to her a day early" by me. I love my wife but if the guys hear this at the station, I'll never hear the end of it, Max thought to himself watching Cora feed the kids. Later that evening they went to Zeek's house for dinner and everyone was talking about what happened yesterday.

Everyone around the table was shocked except Janette who was cheering Cora on. Only Janette would think that kind of foolery was acceptable in public. But I guess you can understand why Cora reacted the way she did. Since Juanita showed up on their honeymoon and on their anniversary 7 yrs later, she got what was due to her. Juanita better take that beating as a warning to leave the Ramirez family alone.

2

New Year, Old Antics

Dec 31st was a day of peace for the officers of Richfield after all of the holiday craziness. Malcolm called Jamal to check on his sister then he facetimed Christian to see his niece. After talking to Rashad and Max for nearly an hour a piece he called Mike to see what his grandmother had been up to. Lastly he called his parents even though he could've just gone next door to talk. Dad, what do you think we'll have to deal with in the field this coming year? To answer your question : a whole lot of weirdness.
Think about it son when each of us started on the force people acted weirder than they did the previous year. You're right about that dad but let's hope people don't

act like or worse than grandma. Boy, nobody can compete with your grandma. After sharing a laugh with his dad Malcolm went to check on his children only to find them in the playroom with their new toys. He was so happy seeing his children playing happily not knowing he was there at all. After an enjoyable final day of 2030 and all the fireworks in the neighborhood it was time for some sleep before heading to the station.

Now it's Jan 1st and time to see all the guys at the station. When he walked and spoke to everyone the first call of the year came in with the report of a stolen car at a construction site. Malcolm and his partner Luis made their way to the site, when they arrived the intoxicated suspect was walking to the corner store. When Malcolm made contact with the suspect to question her she simply said: *I already stole it and I didn't want to resteel it, so I took the keys and came over to the store.* Dumbstruck by what he just heard Malcolm remembered what his dad told him about the new year and the people.

Needless To Say that drunk young lady went to jail and the stolen vehicle was returned to the owner. Before they could make it back toward the station another call came over the radio for a shoplifter at the supermarket. Upon arriving Luis spotted the duo coming out of the west entrance and was in hot pursuit. One of the suspects tried to hit Malcolm with the cart but missed. Once in cuffs the female suspect looked at Malcolm and Luis then yelled " *What we're doing is right and what you're doing is wrong".* To that Luis looked at her and yelled " Uno Reverse".

On the way to lunch Luis glanced over at Malcolm and asked: Have you noticed that for this to be the first day of the year people are stupider than they were last year? With a chuckle Malcolm replied: Forest Gump was right "Stupid is as Stupid does". I can't get over how that lady said that committing crime is right and fighting crime is wrong. What was she ingesting to believe that nonsense, Malcolm thought out loud. I don't even want to find out the answer to that last question,Luis replied.

By the time Malcolm walked into the house his children ran full speed to greet him. Then Kapri greeted him with a kiss when a knock at the door startled them. The family opened the door together to find their new neighbor Chantel standing with a batch of oatmeal raisin cookies and a note. When she left Kapri opened the note to read it;

Malcolm

I just graduated from the academy and will be starting at the station in a week. I was hoping you'd be willing to train me so we could get to know each other better. And who knows what kind of magic we'll make together. I made these cookies for your family and when they're out the way we can be together

Chantel

Walking over to the trashcan Kapri threw the cookies

away. Turning around she looked at Malcolm asking: Did this trick just ask my husband to cheat on me with her? Did she not see me standing at the door with you and our children? Does she think she's going to play stepmom to my kids? Look Malcolm, you and dad need to find her a different partner because she keeps trying my patience. Me and grams will be up there to whoop her butt in front of everyone at that station. You know how extra your grandmother is so this chick needs to be dealt with quickly.

A week later on her first day at the station Chantel got her feelings hurt. Malcolm talked to Zeek, our new police chief to have her train with Laticia, our best female on the force. By the end of the day Laticia reported to Zeek how obsessed this girl is with breaking up Malcolm's marriage. Zeek knew that in order to keep the peace in his station he had to transfer Chantel to another district. So after a week at Richfield station Chantel was sent to Tennessee State to due security.

That just made her angry and vengeful toward Zeek, Malcolm and Kapri. It's one thing to be mad at the Williams men but when it comes to their families you've crossed the line. I don't what Chantel was thinking of walking down the street to bully two little kids minding their own business. That was all the ammunition Kapri needed to defend herself and her kids. At the sound of Kayleigh crying Kapri outside to find Chantel laughing at her crying son and daughter.

Out of nowhere Kapri swung the plate that Chantel had brought the cookies on. When the plate connected with her head Chantel flew off the porch into an electric pole. Kapri marched over to her saying: stay away from my family before the whooping gets worse. Take this as a warning for the future.

Before she could walk away Janette pulled up to the house and got out to inform Chantel of some facts: What you just got wasn't a threat it was a promise of what I do to people like you. We'll come back to this dilemma later in the story.

3

Old Stomping Grounds

By the end of January Mike stopped by the station to visit Zeek and the guys. When he entered the station a call came over the radio of a carjacking in progress and the vehicle description matched Janette's car. Both Mike and Zeek jumped into the patrol car heading to the scene. As they pulled up it was no surprise to see Janette was already beating the suspect up in the street. The two men that loved her dearly just stood there shaking their heads at the sight before them. After 10 minutes Mike walked over to stop Janette while Zeek cuffed the suspect.

Once back at the station Zeek took the suspect to booking while Mike talked to Rashad in the lobby. The next thing they knew a man in a black Adidas track suit walked in demanding money. Rashad and Mike looked at one another in disbelief at this man. Susan the operator was scared at first then she laughed at the fool before her. Of all places to rob you chose a police station in broad daylight, Rashad said to the guy. Then he walked over to put the cuffs on the guy before taking him to booking.

What else will this year bring out of people in this city, Mike thought as he left to go home. When he arrived home Janette was on the porch talking to someone aggressively. As he walked up to the door Mike noticed it was their neighbor Thelma from across the street.What could've happened with these two, Mike thought to himself. At the bottom of the stairs the whole neighborhood could hear Janette yelling.

Janette: 1) How did you get the number to my house? 2) Why are you leaving messages asking my husband to meet up with you after I go to bed? 3) Didn't you get the point when I made you those brownies that made you sick?

Baby, don't make idle threats that will land you in jail? And Thelma don't you say another word because I could have you arrested for harassment. You have no right to be calling my home without our consent, Mike

said angrily. I'm tired of this pettiness between the two of you, you're both grandmothers for Christ sake act your age was all he said before walking into the house.He listened to the messages and recorded them on his phone before erasing them.
Janette stood back watching as her husband before approaching to apologize for her actions. She has never seen her husband reach his limit and go off like that. Maybe this was just what it would take for Janette to change the way she dealt with people, but we'll see if it works. Let's hope she doesn't get into any more trouble around the town. Like I said in the last chapter we'll check back on them later on in the story.

4

I didn't call you, Siri called you

It's now February and Jamal was back in Richfield to celebrate the birthdays of his children. While he was in town he stopped by the station to chat with the guys. A call came in regarding a hit and run just 2 blocks away. Jamal offered to help out since he was there in the area, so he rode with Malcolm to the scene. As they arrived Jamal went to talk to the eye witnesses at the scene. Malcolm spotted the suspect walking back to the scene from the direction of the station.
Sir, can I ask you what happened here since you're bleeding, Malcolm asked. Drunkenly said: Look man I never left the scene but I came back to see what happened here. **Jamal:** So who made the call to the police if none of you did. It was him, a bystander said pointing to the intoxicated suspect. Looking around the unsteady suspect then tells them: I didn't call you, Siri called you from my phone.
Just for that level of stupidity the men had no choice but to arrest the intoxicated man. After getting the man into a cell Malcolm and Jamal shook their heads at what this fool said down the street. After bidding

farewell to the fellas Jamal was making his way back to his children when he noticed a man flagging him down for help. When he pulled over the man asked if he was the police. Jamal replied: Yeah man what can I help you with? The man then gave Jamal the weirdest story he'd ever heard in his life.

Jamal had to call back to the station for one of the officers to come to his location. Once Max arrived Jamal asked the man to tell Max his story again. Max took out his notepad to take notes as the man told his story and this story was a waste of time. **Suspect:** I want to press charges on my dealer for stealing my $25 and not returning with my weed. He ran into that house across the street and won't come out.

Jamal walked to the house to question the occupants who said nobody entered their home at all that day. When Jamal came out to the street the suspect was on the phone with dispatch telling them the same story he'd told Max and Jamal. At this moment Max was annoyed and placed the man under arrest for misuse of 911 and thanked Jamal for his help. No problem man, an officer's job is never done even when your traveling, Jamal replied.

I never knew people could come up with such ridiculous reasons to call the police. We don't have anything like this where I stay in Va. With a chuckle Maax shook his head saying: you saw first hand what we deal with even Chief Byrd's wife will make you question your sanity as a cop. One Day we'll take a trip to your city and see how the people act out there. So have a safe trip home and keep in touch, Max said while getting back into his patrol car with the suspect. After getting on the road to go back to the Stanton residence Jamal shook his head and laughed at the things he's seen in Richfield.

A week later Jamal was at home in Antioch with his two children watching them play in the yard. Harrison asked out of the blue "Daddy can I be a police man when I grow up just like you"? It warmed his heart to know that his son wanted to follow in his footsteps. You sure can buddy was his reply with a smile looking over at his mini me.

5

Crazy drunks in town

Back in Antioch, Va Jamal decided to go out for a relaxing night away from the kids. For the first time in his life Jamal walked into a club. After ordering a drink Jamal sat to the side watching how people conducted themselves and found it hilarious. Some people were trying to start a fight, others were using terrible pickup lines towards women. Out the corner of his eye he noticed a female about to fall off of a stool. Raising over to catch her Jamal sat her in a booth to make sure she was alright.

Her hair was a mess on her head as he tried to get information out of her. After about 15 minutes of her babbling Jamal was able to get her name and address in order to get her an Uber. While waiting for the rideshare Jamal finished his drink and saved her number in his phone. As he was trying to get her into the car the girl tells him "I can't breathe, my hair is blocking my breath". Then Jamal turned to the driver and cancelled the ride and drove her home himself. After making sure the young lady named Sylvia was safely in her home Jamal made his way home as well. The next day Jamal went to his station for his shift when he saw a young woman sitting in the lobby waiting.

Approaching he noticed it was Sylvia which shocked him. Concerned, he asked if everything was ok with her. Everything is fine. I just wanted to thank you for what you did last night, officer Reynolds. Nobody has ever looked out for me like that, can we have coffee or maybe lunch or dinner sometime? Sure Sylvia I have my lunch break at 11:30 so I'll stop by, Jamal told her as he walked her to her car. Throughout his shift Jamal found himself wondering what a friendship with Sylvia would be like.

When 11:30 came Jamal parked at the curb in front of Sylvia's home. After having a lunch of salad and fish tacos Jamal headed back to work. On his way out the door he noticed a man trying to steal a car in her neighbor's driveway. Upon noticing Jamal the man pretended to walk away but turned around and tried to get in the vehicle again. Sylvia came to the door to see what the commotion was in her yard to find Jamal arresting the man.

Upon closer inspection Jamal could tell the man was under the influence of something and he was completely ignoring Jamal's commands. He didn't even notice or care that he was being arrested in broad daylight. Back at the station his co-workers asked what the man was being charged with. Jamal let them know the man was being charged with 2 counts of attempted motor vehicle theft. As he was speaking the man attempted to escape and steal Jamal's patrol car from in front of the station.

For the first time in his law enforcement career Jamal found out that people are crazy everywhere, not just in Richfield, TN. For now we'll let Jamal protect his city and we'll check back with him later on in the story.

6

Spring break in VA

Now it's April and the entire Williams family along with Max and Rashad's families reserved Air B&Bs in Antioch VA. The kids were excited to hang with Serenity and Harrison for a week. After checking in Zeek called Jamal to let him where they were staying. Later that night all the men went to hangout while the ladies took the kids to Aunt Ella's for a few hours.

While out the men went to the same club where Jamal met Sylvia to grab drinks. All the waitresses were flirting with them which made Mike glad Janette didn't know where they were. A fight broke out near the restroom as Max and Rashad walked by. They went over to break it up when a patrend shouted: someone call the police. Max and Rashad replied " We are the Police". Then the men finally after what seemed like forever were able to get the two intoxicated individuals apart.

And then Jamal walked over with two officers from his precinct to take the suspects. Before leaving the officers all asked for statements from both individuals involved. The female wasn't very coherent due to her intoxication. The male on the other hand explained how he stopped buying her drinks and she got angry with everyone at the bar. Are you injured at all sir, Mike asked. Yeah, man she bit my knee and spit in my mouth while we were scrappin on the floor. In utter disbelief of what he'd just heard Zeek turned to Jamal saying: You really this type of stuff only happens in Richfield? Then the two men shared a laugh together before making their way to the exit.

The next day the guys shared the story of their night out. All the ladies were in a fit of tears and laughter at what the woman did to the man's knee and face. I hope that man got tested at a hospital, she may have given him TB, HIV, Hepatitis, Tetanus or Covid, Janette replied wiping her tears. By the middle of the week all the men took the kids out to the park to hang out. Then Max wanted to know if the guys wanted to go to Dave and Busters after they took the kids back to the house.

All the guys agreed and continued to chat about how Jamal is handling the role of being a single dad. It was rough at first and I kept pestering Ms.Ella to the point where I found myself to be a nuisance. Then Jamal turned to Zeek saying: Man how did you do this with 3 kids. I have 2 and I'm so confused by this parenting thing. Shaking his head with a chuckle Zeek replied; I was just like you man but I left it in God's hands. Then

I met Lani and got 3 more so maybe you need to ask God for a helpmate to raise your children. With this encouragement Jamal told the guys about Sylvia and how they met.

On Friday night the girls asked Jamal to bring Sylvia to have dinner with them. While out at the restaurant Harmony and Malcolm talked to Jamal and Sylvia about how much they loved their siblings. Those two siblings were adamant about wanting the best for those two little munchkins. Both Jamal and Sylvia promised to take great care of Serenity and Harrison.

The next night on Saturday all the couple went out one final time before heading back to Richfield. The couples went bowling and to a local diner to eat some dinner. On the way back to the house they stopped at the club. While sitting at the table Cora noticed what she thought was a baby in a car seat at the bar.Guys I think someone brought a baby to the club and it's at the bar, she said to everyone at the table.

On instinct the men went toward the bar just as a woman who clearly was a dancer at the local strip club appeared. She picked up the child who looked to be no older than 3 months old and nearly fell. Jamal caught her just as Mike took the baby from her hands. Then she turns to lock eyes with Zeek saying: I'm so drunk, I almost fell on my back while holding my baby. Everyone within earshot of them burst out into laughter at what she said. Once the young lady was in police custody the baby was taken to the hospital to be checked out.

The next morning before Zeek called Jamal to let him know they were getting ready to head back home. Jamal let him know that Sylvia had started the paperwork last night to adopt the baby. That's great man, it's all "**In the line of duty**"we'll be in touch and if you need our help just call, we got your back, Zeek replied. Thanks man I really appreciate you saying that, Jamal spoke before ending the call.

7

Hilarious Traffic Stop

Now that Spring Break is over and the kids are back in school it was time for the fellas to head back into serving and protecting Richfield,TN. At the station all the guys have a meeting before the start of their shifts. Meanwhile Mike who is retired is out at JCPenney to buy Janette a gift. After getting a charm bracelet and some lingerie Mike was heading back to the house when he noticed a car driving erratically across the road.

He motioned for the car to pull over so he could make sure the occupant was ok. As he approached the vehicle the female in the driver's seat looked to be in shock. Mike called to the station where Rashad answered the call. What's going on chief, is grams in trouble again, he asked? She's good but I need whoever is on patrol by the mall to come over to MLK Blvd. There's a woman on the side of the road slumped over the front seat.

Chief, I'll let Malcolm know to head your way and the ambulance is enroute. Once he hung up Mike went over to the vehicle again as the young lady began to stir. Sluggishly getting out of the car the young lady spoke in slurs saying;You called for backup because I have no teeth. This surprised Mike who replied: I called for help because I'm concerned about your health. Ma'am you almost hit me swerving down the road.

Once the young lady was checked by EMS she was taken into custody for Drug Possession and DUI. By May Max and Rashad were on night patrol when they noticed a car rolling slowly with its lights off. The vehicle was heading toward the street of Malcolm and Zeek's home. They followed at a distance until they were 2 doors down when Chantel got out of the car walking toward Malcolm's house. Max called Malcolm and put the call on speaker.**Malcolm:**Hey Max what's up man?**Max:** Are you home man?**Malcolm:** No; I'm at the station with my dad, why?**Rashad:** Man Chantel is at your house, I think she's gonna break in to harm your family.

Malcolm: with a chuckle replied, she can do that if she wants to. She's got a surprise waiting on the other side of the door. **Rashad:** What surprise you got in there, some traps setup? **Malcolm:** My grandmother is in there with Kapri and the kids. **Max:** Well at least I know this night on patrol will be good. After hanging up Chantel was on the porch attempting to pick the lock. As the men got out of the car Janette opened the door to a shocked Chantel. Then Kapri stepped out the door and closed it behind her just as Janette asked

"who are you heifer"?
Grams, this is the neighbor I was telling you is trying to ruin my marriage. So you are the one causing all that stress at the station for my grandson. Well he would be better with me instead of her was all Chantel could get out before Janette went on the attack. Slapping Chantel so hard that her head bounced off the railing and she rolled to the sidewalk. Walking down the stairs Janette and Kapri looked like two hungry lions stalking their prey. Max and Rashad moved closer just as Kapri was about to slap Chantel. Max placed cuffs on Chantel announcing she was under arrest for (burglary, harassment, stalking and attempted murder).

Janette, being extra as usual, went to inspect the car Chantel was driving. What's this powder in this glove box, Janete yelled out? 1)Are you on crack 2) were you gonna poison my grandbabies and their mother3) did you think you were gonna be with my grandson? Then she went to the trunk where she found a suitcase saying: so you were packed to escape after harming my family? Opening the suitcase Janette finds photos of the family and love letters addressed to Malcolm. Both the men felt bad for Malcolm and his family because he knows what it's like having a stalker.

8

Unofficial Officer Janette

If you remember last month Mike bought Janette some gifts at the mall. Well after the guys told him about her searching Chantel's car for other evidence. Mike called a jeweler asking for a custom police badge for his wife that read "Unofficial Officer Byrd". I swear that woman should've been a cop on the force, he thought to herself.

On Mother's Day Mike was giving Janette her gifts when she saw that badge and she lost her mind. Then Mike started to regret having it made for her. She now thinks she is a member of the force and went down to the station flashing your badge at all the guys. "Pop, why would you buy that for her knowing how dramatic she is"? Zeek, listen son it was part of a costume for us to roll play in the house. I didn't think she'd wear it outside the house and really think she's a cop,Mike said sincerely.

This is a lesson well learned by Michael Byrd to never involve Janette in anything that has to do with the law or Law Enforcement. Just as she was leaving the station there was a robbery in progress at the bank down the street. Janette went in the direction of the bank and all of the guys followed her there. Upon arriving Janette walked in and stood by the door watching the robbers movements. As the robber tried to get past her she tripped him and took the money back up to the counter. Meanwhile Malcolm and Zeek took the man into custody.

For the rest of the month of May Janette believed she was really a cop. Everytime she left the house this woman was looking for some crime to solve by herself. It hasn't registered with her that looking for trouble isn't how you solve crime. Even when she goes to work at the hospital she wears that badge and tells everyone she's also part of security.What are we gonna do with this woman is the biggest question on the minds of everyone in the city.

Even Zeek called Jamal and Dr.Matthews to share the news of Mike creating a monster that everyone has to deal with. Those were two hilarious conversations and Zeek definitely needed to laugh at his mother. We'll check back in with our pretend officer again later on to see what she's up to.

9

Summer Vacation Crime

With the kids out of school the whole crew decided to go to the beach for two weeks. During the trip to their beach house Kahlani called Ramona and Jean to talk about Janette's antics. Nobody could keep a straight face listening to the stories. Kahlani had the call on speaker so her parents could talk to everyone in the van. **Jean:** Mike I know you meant well and didn't expect this to be the outcome. **Mike:** I'm glad you said that man because that therapy we had last year was a waste. **Ramona:** Didn't the doctor tell you there was no hope for my friend. **Janette:** That's because there is nothing wrong with me.
Ramona: Friend you are a mess but we love you just the way you are. **Janette:** Thank you friend for that vote of confidence. Then Kahlani said goodbye to her parents before hanging up. The family made it to their rental property and got settled in . It was 4pm by this time so it was time to feed the kids. All the ladies except Janette were in the kitchen making food for the group. After everyone ate and the kids played awhile it was time for bed.

The next day the group went down to the boardwalk to do some activities with the children. Just as they arrived at the boardwalk Juanita and Samantha who are Max and Rashad's stalkers grab Lincoln and Kaitlyn. As they turned to flee Janette stepped up punching both in the face. Completely folded over in pain the two women held their bloody noses while being belittled by other patrends for attempted kidnapping.

While waiting for the local police to arrive Regina and Cora each got a chance to vent their frustrations. In the blink of an eye both of these moms went on the attack against the two women who have been harassing their families. Once the men got their wife's under control the police arrived and took statements from everyone before taking the two women away. The kids weren't deterred at all and still wanted to see the attractions on the boardwalk.

After 4 hrs at the boardwalk the group went back to their rental. All of the ladies were still upset by the incident of the day. After dinner and getting the children into bed each couple prayed together before going to bed. For the rest of the time there all of the men talked with the local police regarding charges against the suspects. We already know that Juanita is being charged with kidnapping and escaping from jail. Samantha was charged with kidnapping for her role in the crime.

After their two weeks at the beach was over and they

made their way home all the school kids went to camp. For their anniversary Christian and Desiree decided to stay in with their 9 month old. A call came from the hospital asking if they were available to work a shift? Kapri told them 1) today is our wedding anniversary and 2) I'm on maternity leave so No we will not be available to work tonight. Christian was proud of his wife for standing up for her family.

The next day Christian went into the hospital where he was approached by a nurse named Chelsea who has a crush on him. Chelsea asked if he would have lunch with her today? No; Chelsea I will not and can not have lunch with you, Christian stated. Why am I not pretty enough for you to be seen with? Chelsea, there is nothing wrong with your looks, it's because 1)I'm a married man 2) it's my wedding anniversary 3) my wife also works here at this hospital 4) I'm not going to cheat on my wife just because you're in love with me. 5) I'm only going to have lunch with my wife.

By 1pm Christian went home to have lunch with his wife and daughter. As he sat down to eat the phone rang and Desiree answered it. Chelsea was on the other end saying that she and Christian were in a relationship and had sex while at work today. Chelsea must be slow or really stupid to not care that he was on speaker the whole time. Christian lets her know that he is going to HR about her harassing Kapri and trying to ruin his marriage. After hearing this Chelsea hung up and went back to work.

The following day Desiree left Christiana with Kahlani before heading to the hospital. Once at the hospital Desiree made her way to the HR office where Christian and Chelsea were seated. Once she was seated next to her husband their meeting began. Chelsea showed a picture of herself having relations with another doctor at the hospital but claimed it was Christian. The HR rep informed her that the person in the photo wasn't but was Deonte. And how do you figure that's Deonte, Chelsea asked, playing dumb.

Desiree looked over annoyed and replied, "because Deonte like the man in these photos has dreads and My husband has a bald fade". Then the HR rep called Deonte into the office asking him about their affair to which he confirmed as true. The rep told them they were terminated and to leave the premises immediately. Then he announced that he and Chelsea were expecting a child but she wants everyone to believe that Christian is the father so Desiree will leave him. After hearing this the HR rep called the police and Max and Malcolm showed up. They arrested Chelsea for harassment and attempted entrapment.

10

Breaking the Law

With two weeks until school starts all of our boys in blue need to be ready. Y'all know the crime rate can go either way in the city. Aug 20th was a quiet day until a call came in about a break-in at Malcolm's home. The neighbors reported seeing a person 5'5 slender in size snooping around the house at 2pm. Within 10 minutes the room that Marquis and Kayleigh shared went up in flames. Thankfully nobody was home when it happened.
At 2:30 Zeek,Malcolm and the fire department arrived at the house fire. They waited outside as the arson investigators did their job. By 3:15 the investigators let them know that the fire was intentional and handed Malcolm a laminated note left in the crime scene. He didn't even have to read it to know who did it. Without looking Malcolm let out a tired sigh and told Zeek: Dad I know who the suspect is.
Zeek: Who would try to kill you son, you don't have any beef with anybody in the streets do you?
Malcolm: Only one person wants my wife and children dead out of jealousy

The two looked at each other and said in unison "Chantel". Zeek called in an APB (All Points Bulletin) for any officers out on patrol. 2hrs later Chantel was arrested at the station when she arrived for her shift. Her charges included Arson and Premeditated murder and attempted murder. Thank God Kapri was at the shop finishing a client's hair and the kids were in daycare when the crime occurred or Chantel would be charged with triple murder. For the next month the whole neighborhood banded together to fix Malcolm's house for him.

On the first day back to school Aug 20th Max and Rashad were stopping at Citco to gas up their patrol car when they heard the call over the radio about a robbery in progress where they were. **Rashad:** Man, let's surprise the suspect when they exit. **Max:** Sounds good to me bro. They each stood in front of the two exits of the store when the two suspects ran straight into them head first.

After cuffing the suspects Rashad returned the money to the cashier. Then he went to pump his fuel when the manager came to the car telling the officers that he was paying for their fuel today. Now instead of being in school these two young men were going to juvie for armed robbery. **Max:** Bro, are we doing something wrong in our lives? Here I thought we were being role models to the kids in the hood. And they choose to commit crime and go to juvie rather than follow our lead. **Rashad :**I know man it really saddens me too but we can't give up on them yet. All we can do is keep trying to get through to them.

The second week of school a call came into the station about a shooting at the daycare that Christiana was in. Zeek,Malcolm,Rashad, Max and Michael all made their way to the scene. The scene was very bloody with the bodies of 6 children and 2 deceased daycare workers. The sound of loud cries lead Zeek to his granddaughter in the nursery still in her crib. The 1 yr old had been grazed on her shoulder by the bullet that was lodged in the wall behind the crib. Once the scene was secured Zeek and Michael went to the hospital with Christiana where her parents work.

After babygirl was checked out, Zeek took her home to hangout with Kahlani until her parents got off of work.Max met them at the station to watch some surveillance footage of the suspect. They didn't recognize the female in the video so they sent a text of the young lady to Christian and Desiree to see if they knew her. Within 5 minutes they both text back that her name was Chelsea Nelson, a nurse that was fired from the hospital.

What is with these crazy women going to jail for attempted murder of innocent children. What makes them really believe the man they're in love with will give them the time of day after she kills his family? Any man that is willing to go along with one of these crazy women is a bigger fool than Jamal was with Zeek's baby mamas. I hope Chelsea gets some help and finds someone who will truly love her.

We'll check on her later on in the story to see how she's coping with rejection. Because Christian and Desiree have a lot of backup in Law Enforcement as Chelsea has found out.

11

Pop Pop lays down the Law

At home Michael was waiting for Janette to come downstairs so they could go to Zeek's house. Just as they stepped out the door Michael could smell smoke. When he turned toward the driveway he noticed one of their neighbors Elizabeth near the tailpipe of Janette's car. "What are you doing next to my wife's car Liz"? Oh nothing just tying my shoe, she replied with a wink before attempting to walk away.
Come over here for a second Liz, I have something to say to you in front of my wife, Michael replied. Batting her eyelashes at him Liz strutted up the walkway. Before Michael could get a word out Janette's car exploded in flames. The entire neighborhood came

out to see what the commotion was. After everyone surrounded the house Mike had an announcement to make to them.

Mike: I need to explain something to each and every one of you. This woman to my left is my wife and you can and will respect her. If you don't you'll have to suffer her wrath and I can't save you. It's my duty to protect this neighborhood but I will not tolerate any of these antics like this is unacceptable. Elizabeth if you had killed my wife in that car, the chief of police would be arresting you for killing his mother.

All of the women on the block were in shock by what they just heard Mike say. None of them knew Janette and Mike were Zeek's parents. Just as the fire fighters were finishing putting out the fire Malcolm pulled up to the scene. **Malcolm:** Grandma, what happened here? Are you hurt? Do you need the EMT's? Just firing off questions as he walked up onto the porch. Janette just stood there in shock looking at what used to be her car. **Malcolm:** Pop Pop what happened here that's got grandma so quiet? **Mike:** Scanning the crowd he said grandson, Elizabeth here tried to kill your grandmother by blowing up her car. At the sound of this information Malcolm walked over to arrest Elizabeth for Arson and Attempted Murder.

Elizabeth: Mike I'm sorry don't let him take me to jail. I Love You and you know I wouldn't do anything to harm you ever. Before he left Malcolm had words for the crowd as well. **Malcolm:** You all see what I am doing right now and if you want to join her in lockup I will come back to arrest you. Do not try to harm either of my grandparents. Once he was gone the couple got into Mike's truck and rode to Zeek's home.

In October Mike and Janette walked into the Dodge dealership to look at some cars. After an hour Janette chose a 2024 Dodge Durango with 9000 miles. Turning to Mike she says "baby I love it, can we get it"? Of course my queen let's sign the paperwork so you can drive it home. In the office Janette asked for the manager because she didn't like the way the saleswoman was looking at Mike. Once the paperwork was done Janette told the manager that he should keep an eye on the sales lady they worked with.

12

The case of stolen identity

By the first of November there is a list of crimes being committed around town. The weird part is the suspect is claiming to be Janette Byrd. With video footage of the suspect it was clear to everyone at the station that they didn't need to arrest Janette. A screenshot of the suspect was displayed on the news asking for help identifying her.
In 48 hrs the manager at the dealership called into the station with a full description of the suspect. He even did his own investigation of the young lady acting suspicious after Mike and Janette left with their vehicle. The manager also told dispatch that she was at the dealership at that very moment. Sandra turned to

face Zeek telling him everything the manager said. Zeek turned to Malcolm and motioned for him to join him for the ride.

With a nod Malcolm got into the passenger seat and headed to the dealership.The manager told them that the young woman was named Adonna Lynn Michaels and handed them some paperwork.**Malcolm:** What is this your handing me, sir? **Manager:** This is the paperwork that Mr&Mrs Byrd signed for the vehicle. The other form is for a bank loan of $19,000 with a forged signature of Mrs. Byrd. Here is a checkbook for an account opened in Mrs. Byrd's name.

Zeek: Thank You for gathering all of this information for our case. Where is she right now,sir? **Manager:** She's in my office right this way gentlemen. When the door opened Adonna was in awe of the two handsome men that walked in with her boss. **Malcolm:** We'll need you to stand up and put your hands behind your back. **Adonna:** What's going on, why am I under arrest? Not in the mood for her innocent act Malcolm replied: For someone who has committed (Identity Theft,Bank Fraud and Forgery) you sure are stupid.

Zeek: You are too young and short to be my mother. My mother is 70 yrs old, 5'8 and 175 lbs. Why would you assume the identity of an elderly woman anyway? With no remorse Adonna stated: because I want that man but either of you two fine officers will do. All the way to the station the father and son shook their heads. What is with all this fatal attraction going on in this city?

As Janette would say: all these lonely women with no ambition waiting for a man to take care of them. Of all the men in this city they only want the men in the Williams Family. All because of this little heifer Janette had no Thanks to be Giving on Nov 25th. For the first time in this series she had nothing to say while visiting her family. That was very concerning to everyone "was Janette about to have a breakdown", Mike thought sitting next to her in the living room.

I guess all Janette needed was for someone to attack her personally to calm her down. Not just flirting with her husband or one of the men in her family.

Everytime she looks at her new car all she can do is shake her head at what she has endured in the past month. Let's hope this has been able to help Janette with how she deals with others.

13

Snow in the City

Here we are at the end of the year and there's a chill in the air. Not just the chill of the 34 degree weather condition but the vindictive revenge people have toward this family. After all that's happened throughout this story so far it makes you wonder what these scrooges have in store for our officers?
On Dec 1st Zeek was in the station alone so he decided to call Jamal to see how things are in VA. **Zeek:** How is everything in antioch, man? Hopefully not as crazy as it is here in Richfield. **Jamal:** Me and the kids along with Sylvia and Aunt Ella are doing good over here. But tell me is it true someone tried to steal your moms identity? With a laugh Zeek answered "Yeah, man."
Jamal: That's crazy, why would somebody do that?
Zeek: It's simple man, Jealousy. Some other lady tried to kill my mom but all she did was blow up her car. And get this some crazy woman shot my granddaughter because she's in love with Christian.
Jamal: You have to be kidding bro. She shot a 1 yr old I can't believe that. Nevermind I can believe it because you have all the good-looking people in your family

while the rest of us are trying to catch up.
Zeek: Man, shut up just because nobody is after you, you're safe. You are a cop and your girl is a nurse. Go to the post office we sent stuff for the kids since we won't be able to travel there this month. **Jamal:** I will and Zeek,I appreciate everything you do for my kids. And I'm sorry for the part I played in your stress back in 2020. **Zeek:** It's All good man, all is forgiven on my end.Be safe and be good to those babies.
Once the call ended Jamal sat and reflected on the words Zeek had spoken to him. Zeek and I are in the same age bracket but he talks more like the father I wish I had growing up, he thought to himself. Meanwhile back in Richfield Zeek watched the snowflakes fall at a steady pace while on patrol. Just as he turned onto his street there was a car accident in front of his home. As he crept closer in his truck the sight of his daughter-in-law holding his granddaughter while being pinned under the tire of a car in her driveway scared him. Behind the wheel of the car was Chantel who revved the engine and smiled.
"Chantel, how did you get out of jail?" Zeek asked, outraged by her actions. Oh hi chief my parents posted my bail a week ago she replied looking straight ahead. Kapri was barely conscious but holding on to the sound of her daughter's cries. Swiftly Zeek reached into the window snatching the key fob while putting the car in park.
Quickly he pulled Chantel out of the vehicle placing

her in cuffs just as Malcolm, Rashad and Max arrived. They did a full search for any weapons on the body of the suspect. Once she was in the patrol car all the guys and some neighbors lifted the car so Malcolm could get his family out. To everyone's horror, baby Kayleigh's left leg was crushed and Kapri's right arm was crushed and she was still unconscious. Malcolm was completely distraught as the snow began to pile up around him sticking to the ground. Zeek walked back over to the patrol car to speak to Chantel.

You are a complete disgrace to our profession Chantel and if my daughter-in-law dies you'll never see the light of day, Zeek yelled before slamming the door. Due to the weather conditions Malcolm and Zeek were airlifted to the hospital with Kapri and Kayleigh. At the hospital Christian and Desiree were waiting to see who was coming in. The sight before them was heartbreaking but Christian and Desiree had a job to do and was to save lives.

2 hrs later Christian and Desiree walked into the waiting room where Zeek and Malcolm were sitting stoically. Desiree spoke first saying: Hey Mal just as he looked up to notice them. **Malcolm:** Hey sis how is my baby girl doing? **Desiree:** She's fine, her left leg is broken. She'll be in a cast for 6-8 weeks until it heals, she's sleeping right now. With a nod of his head Malcolm replied OK. Then he turned to Christian asking "how is my wife, bro?"

Christian: Taking a breath he replied somberly: 4 of

her ribs are broken and her right arm is broken as well. I found some bleeding on the brain most likely caused from the point of impact being sandwiched between the cars. She's still unconscious and all we can do is wait to see if she wakes up tomorrow. **Malcolm:** I can't lose her bro, she's my life partner. **Christian:** I know bro and I'll do all I can to give her back to you. Then he turned to Desiree asking "baby can you go get Kayleigh and bring her to room 303 please?"
Sitting in the room Zeek held his sleeping granddaughter while Malcolm held Kapri's limp hand. Baby come back to me please, Marquis and I are worried about you don't leave us. I'm begging you. Just hearing his son's tearful plea reminded Zeek of all the pleas he'd made to his baby mamas in the past. He knows what this moment is like personally from experience. Sending up a prayer asking God to send her back to her family right here in this room.

14

A wish upon a star

After 2 weeks in the hospital and a whole lot of prayers the swelling has gone down on Kapri's brain. This was a miracle for Malcolm because he'd surely quit working in Law Enforcement if he had to bury his wife of 7 years. Once the snow had melted and the roads were safe Kahlani brought Marquis to see his mother for the first time. The young man walked over and held his mother's hand then glanced out the window as a shooting star went across the sky.
I wish my mom would open her eyes, he silently prayed staring out the window. Then he took a seat next to his father who was holding his sister. Dad, I made a wish on a shooting star that mommy will wake up, Marquis said. Thank you buddy we definitely need that wish to come true, Malcolm replied somberly. On the 24th a miracle appeared before them when Kapri finally opened her eyes.
Marquis was the first to notice when he excitedly said: Dad my wish came true, look at mom. Kayleigh crawled herself up into her mother's arm to cuddle saying,mommy you have a cast just like me. It took a

few minutes for Kapri to recognize all the faces around her bed. Seeing his sister-in-law awake made Christian proud to be a medical professional.

The next morning the family went home to the sight of everyone they know in their living room. Each person offered to help out with the two injured ladies of this family. This is literally and figuratively what the definition of Love is as a whole. Kapri has never had this in her life even when it was just her and her mother in a small apartment on the westside of Richfield.

Out of nowhere Janette made her grand entrance with Mike carrying bags of food. "Girl I heard what happened to you and great grandbaby." Are you feeling alright?Do you need any help around the house? Me and Pop Pop will stay to help you guys out, Janette rambled in front of everyone. The whole family was happy to see Janette showing so much care and concern for others. Out of nowhere Janette started telling the story of Adonna stealing her identity.

Kapri had to stop her real quick from retelling that story because the whole state knew the story already. Grams we already know the guys told us and it's been on the news for the world to see, Harmony answered. Well do you know what I would've done to this psycho that tried to hurt Kapri and Kayleigh? Grams what could you possibly have done to Chantel, Malcolm asked.

It's simple, I'd do what I did on the way here tonight. Pop, what did she do tonight,Zeek asked. **Mike:** While we were waiting for the food at World Tavern a drunk lady tried to rob us. Out of nowhere Janette started punching the girl while doing her own version of Mirandaizing her. All the staff were laughing so hard that the food got cold and they had to remake it. **Malcolm:** What kind of rights did you read to the suspect grandma?

Janette: With every hit she was told; *You have the right to go to sleep. Any and every nightmare you have will be staring me. You have a right to not remember any of this beating if you want to. Any and every time I see you it will be on sight.* With that she was out cold on the pavement so,I got back in the car while everyone was laughing.

Everyone of the officers in attendance were on the floor in a fit of laughter over these Miranda rights. **Max:** Grams you are the G.O.A.T, I'll make up my own rights depending on the crime being committed. **Rashad:** Grams you didn't even give the opinion for a lawyer. **Janette:** Why would I do that when she wouldn't even remember when she wakes up. So by the time she wakes up tomorrow she won't even know how she got to lock up.

As we can all see nothing will stop Janette from taking the law into her hands. Where there is disrespect

Janette Byrd will be there to lay a beatdown on the suspect. Maybe she should've been a cop in a past life. You'd think that after all the mess these officers have endured this year but it's not over yet.

15

Closing out 2031

Here we are Dec 31st back in Antioch, VA to check on Officer Jamal Reynolds. Zeek gave him a call and was surprised that he already knew about what had taken place in Richfield. **Jamal:** Man can't believe someone was crazy enough to steal the identity of your mom. And someone tried to kill 2 of your grandchildren along with your daughter-in-law. How are they holding up, man? **Zeek:** Christiana is a happy toddler, she was just grazed by the bullet. Kayleigh is fortunate it was only a broken leg from being pinned under the tire. Kapri isn't handling it well so we're on round the clock watch. She has a broken arm and a small concussion.
Jamal: I don't if I could be professional if someone tried to harm my kids. Zeek you're a better man than me dealing with all this craziness. Man you've had more crime in that city involving your family than we've faced in our entire careers. **Zeek:** Yeah man that's true but don't think someone isn't out there

waiting to get at you. But if something happens to those kids just Malcolm and I will be there to help.

Jamal: I appreciate all the guys, even chief for putting up with your mom.

Zeek told Jamal about Janette's version of the Miranda rights and the two men shared a hearty laugh. After the call ended Jamal went to see what his children were doing. Entering their room he found Sylvia playing along with the baby girl she adopted. She named the little girl Kiara Janae and was glad to have saved this child from a bad situation.

Then his cell rang with a call from the station regarding a DUI case in his neighborhood. Once Jamal had finished his call there was a loud crash outside. Rushing outside he found a young woman injured from a gunshot to the chest and her sedan crashed into his neighbors truck. Just like the title of this book " In the line of duty" Jamal jumped into action calling for help. Officer Reynolds originally planned to propose to Sylvia not be solving crime on the eve of 2032. Once the scene was secured and the young lady was safely taken to the hospital he went on with his original plan.

Meanwhile back in Richfield Zeek was at home with his family getting ready to watch the fireworks display in the park. Out of nowhere the sound of gunfire erupted on the corner and on instinct to protect their family Malcolm and Zeek leaped into action. As they approached the corner the father and son came face to face with a terrible sight. A young mother and a toddler were shot and the intoxicated man aiming the gun at them.

After getting the man in cuffs onlookers provided care to the victims. When the ambulance arrived and the victims were taken to the local hospital it was time for questioning. Y'all won't believe who did the questioning yup it was Janette since the male suspect wouldn't talk to the police. 1) Why did you shoot the young lady at the park? 2) Did you really have to shoot the baby? 3) What did the child do to you, fool? 4) Do you know what you really deserve for the crime you committed today? All the men stood back to let Janette do her thang. Then the suspect opened his mouth and began to speak to Janette in a very non-emotional tone.

Suspect: With a blank stare spoke as follows: (I) Bernard Lee Jenkins shot Tahierria LaShae Jenkins and Lawrence Ashton Jenkins. I shot my wife and son for personal reasons. The reasons were that she planned to divorce me for cheating with my employer's wife. She threatened to take my son away from me. Now my son deserved those bullets for telling me he didn't love me anymore. To answer your question old lady,I don't care what you think I deserve for shooting them.

That was all it took for Janette to snap, nobody calls Janette OLD and not get these hands. In 2.5 seconds Janette was over that table reading the man his rights only in Janette fashion. *"You have the right to shut up, anything you say can and will get you knocked out cold. You have the right to pretend to not hear me. The next punch you take will either make you hear me or make you totally deaf. With those rights in mind, do you plan to be more respectful toward me".*

Malcolm: With a chuckle said "Grandma you didn't even offer the man a choice to get a lawyer". **Janette:** Grandson ain't no lawyer gonna defend what he did to his wife and child. That's why I didn't mention the option of a lawyer. You better hope your brother and sister-in-law can save the two of them because this fool is looking at 2 Life Sentences for double homicide. **Zeek:** She's right son, we need to put him back in his cell and get to the hospital. Max, Shad can you take him to his cell and meet us at the hospital.

20 minutes later all of the officers were gathered at the hospital to talk to Christian and Desiree. **Desiree:** The child has lost a lot of blood and will need a transfusion to survive. He was shot in the back so the bullet ripped through his kidney and lodged in the spleen. We stopped the internal bleeding and put him on a respirator until we get a blood donor. **Christian:** As for mom, she's in surgery right now. She was shot in the shoulder and in the head. He was really trying to execute her. I'll keep you posted on her progress after the surgery.

On the way out of the hospital Zeek received a call from Jamal about a case. **Zeek:** What's up with you man? **Jamal:** There was a car crash in front of my

house this morning and the victim told me some news about the suspect that you need to know. **Zeek:** What do we need to know out here? **Jamal:** My victim told me that she's pregnant by a guy named Bernard Lee Jenkins and he's the one that shot her this morning and was headed your way to be with his wife.
Zeek: We got him in custody here already, man. That fool shot his wife and son down the street from my house. The son needs a blood transfusion to survive and his wife is in surgery to remove the bullet from her brain. **Jamal:** So it's a double murder case here and possibly a second double murder out there with the same suspect. This is crazy man. But I wanted to tell you that Sylvia and I are engaged.
Zeek: Yeah, man this is quite the coincidence for us to have overlapping cases with the same suspect. But on a lighter note Congrats on the engagement, I'll let the guys know. We'll come down to plan your bachelor party after these two cases are closed. **Jamal:** I appreciate that a whole lot man, talk to you later. After the call ended Zeek turned to Malcolm to give him the news about their suspect. Then they made their way home to their families and bring in the new year.

16

Conclusion

At the end of this year of fun we'll check in with each of these fine officers. Each of them have shown us their resilience **In the line of duty** throughout this story. We even have another wedding in this saga of Leaving Trauma Behind. We'll take a journey through Jamal's life in the next book **"A Father's Redemption"**. But for now let's see how each of these officers bought in 2032.
Jamal: Now this man has finally found true love with a great woman. His children are happy and healthy and surrounded by Love. The case against Bernard L Jenkins was coming to an end with the judge handing him 2 Life sentences. All of the crime in Antioch is at a low for the first time in 10 years.
Now all he has on his plate is planning his wedding to Sylvia and welcoming Kiara Janae into his family. Nothing could be better in his life at this point.Let's hope he continues on the right path in life.

Zeek: With this year over our new Police Chief is finally getting some peace. With Bernard behind bars it was time to check on his two victims. At the hospital Christian informed him that the baby was fine. But the mom had died during surgery. So now Bernard has a third Life sentence to his name.
At this point Chief Williams can relax for a little while. He's also preparing to celebrate the engagement of a fellow comrade over in VA. And he'll always have the comedic relief of his mother to make life entertaining. Lastly his 6 children, 5 grandchildren and friends and we can't forget about his god babies (Lincoln, Alexander, Theresa and Kaitlyn). Since he was a child all Zeek wanted to do was serve and protect his city. Throughout this series Zeek has done just that with his head held high as a leader.
Malcolm: This young man has lived out his dreams of following in his dads footsteps. Taking on the role of serving and protecting his city behind his father who is now the Police Chief. As well as being a role model for his siblings and his children. He's proven to be a great husband to Kapri.
The city respects what the men of the Williams Family stand for. Malcolm like Zeek are examples of inspirations for those who share the same dreams in urban communities. We love how Malcolm took the heart and spirit of a warrior that Zeek implemented into his children and used it for good. The way Malcolm shows concern for his ½ sister Serenity since

she was born can melt anyone's heart. And let us not forget about his problem named Chantel. She's not getting out anytime soon due to her 25 yr sentence with a chance at parole in 15 yrs.

Rashad: Now this officer is living comfortably with his wife and son. He's trying to convince Regina to have another child but we'll see how that goes. Since his stalker got the beating of her life at the hands of his wife life is quiet. His son is having the time of his life growing up in a stable happy family. Hopefully nobody tries to interrupt their family anytime soon. Hopefully the crime in the city doesn't get too crazy throughout the city.

Max: This officer is still laughing at how Cora snapped and layed that whoopin down on Juanita. "God knows I love and married the right woman." he relays to himself every morning before leaving for his shift. Having great friends from the academy to the field is even better. His triplets make him proud to be a parent in this cruel world.

Michael: As a retired Police Chief who still loves the city of Richfield. In his spare time he loves to help out at the station where his son is now the Chief. The best part of his life has to be his marriage to the most hilarious woman in town. Buying her a costume to spice up their bedroom now has her believing she's above the law. Nobody can understand how this man can put up with Janette. To be around someone like Janette would drive people insane.
Michael Byrd is a great human being for putting up with her. But this poor guy has his hands full with one , yet their home is a happy one.

Janette: Y'all I'm so happy to help these handsome men of this family. I know people think my line of questioning of others is a little crazy, but sometimes you have to stop being polite and get straight to the point. Everybody knows I have limited patience for stupid people anyway. Before I leave Imma tell you a piece of information about Mike and I. In ***The ByrdSong Diaries*** you guys will find me singing like a canary voicing my opinions about the people in this world. Mike will be the good cop in that series telling me how to deal with people. Y'all know I'm gonna do things my way but I respect my husband's opinion on everything.

Authors Note

After writing this story I have a newfound respect for officers of the law. As well as the issues they come up against in these streets. I took more of a comical approach to telling this story so you can see that cops aren't always serious or aggressive. I also want to thank our local and Statewide Police for all that they do. All those who are joining the Police force, keep fighting a good fight. Don't get caught up in any corrupt activities that will derail your future.

Get ready for the story of Jamal Reynolds who got caught up and derailed his career for 5 years. A Father's Redemption is his journey through the police force to prison and single fatherhood.

Sample of book 13

It's a brisk May morning in 2025 Jamal Reynolds walked out of the Tennessee State Prison. The first thought was his children that he had yet to meet. There was no watching them be delivered, no seeing their first steps, trips to daycare, late night feedings etc. Now it's time to rebuild his life and a relationship with them.

Follow/Contact Me

E-mail: *relatablefictionwriting@gmail.com*
Facebook: *nakeialdavis-moore*
Instagram:*soultavern_ owner2020*
Tik Tok: *LeavingTraumaBehind4*
X:*LeavingTrauma4*

www.ingramcontent.com/pod-product-compliance
Lightning Source LLC
LaVergne TN
LVHW052003060526
838201LV00059B/3813